For my 'little' brother, Rob ~ S S

To 'Smelly Peter – The Great Pea Eater', who would probably have loved to have Percy as a pet! ~ J D

Library of Congress
Cataloging-in-Publication Data
Smallman, Steve.
Little stinker / Steve Smallman ;
[illustrations] Joelle Dreidemy.
p. cm.
Summary: Percy is a little fish who causes a lot of mischief with the foul-smelling bottom bubbles he blows, but just as the other underwater creatures are applauding a hermit crab's revenge, they discover a benefit to Percy's bad habit.
ISBN 978-1-56148-709-7 (hardcover : alk. paper)
[1. Stories in rhyme. 2. Flatulence--Fiction.
3. Fishes--Fiction. 4. Behavior--Fiction.]
I. Dreidemy, Joelle, ill. II. Title.
PZ8.3.S6358Lit 2011
[E]--dc22
2010031235

Copyright © 2011 by Good Books,
Intercourse, PA 17534
International Standard Book Number:
978-1-56148-709-7
Library of Congress Catalog Card Number: 2010031235
All rights reserved. No part of this book may be reproduced in any manner, except for brief quotations in critical articles or reviews, without permission.
Text copyright © Steve Smallman 2011
Illustrations copyright © Joëlle Dreidemy 2011
Original edition published in English by Little Tiger Press, an imprint of Magi Publications,
London, England, 2011
LTP/1500/0134/0910 • Printed in Singapore

Little Stinker!

Steve Smallman   Joëlle Dreidemy

Intercourse, PA 17534
800/762-7171
www.GoodBooks.com

Percy was a little fish,

　　he wasn't smart or sporty.

He wasn't sweet and kind,

　　in fact he could be rather naughty!

Flashy fins and sparkly scales,

　　Percy hadn't got 'em.

But he was VERY good

　　at blowing bubbles . . .

...with his

bottom!

Percy's special bubbles often got him into trouble.

It's easy to make mischief with a well-timed bottom bubble!

He liked to lie in wait as all the fish went swimming past...

Then flip them upside down with an enormous

bottom blast!

At school he always tried to cheat whenever they had races

By blowing stinky bubbles in the other fishes' faces.

Then using supersonic bottom-burping bubble power,

He'd shoot off like a ROCKET at a hundred miles an hour!

Sometimes during class he used to wait for Mrs. Trout

To turn her back and then he'd let a whiffy whopper out!

Then sneakily he'd use his tail to waft the beastly bubble
Behind poor Penny Pufferfish to get her into trouble.

One day a poor old hermit crab was reeling from the smell

Of the bubbly little "present" Percy'd left inside his shell.

"That rotten **little stinker!**" cried the crab.

"Oh, what a pong!

"Hey, Percy!" the crab shouted.

"If you think that you're so clever,

Why don't you try to blow the biggest

bottom bubble EVER?"

Percy's face went purple from the pressure as he tried it.
Then, **BLAAARP!**
he blew a **HUGE** one...

. . . and the crab pushed him inside it!

"It worked!" he shouted.

"Look—that trumpy troublemaker's trapped!"

And all the other underwater creatures

cheered and clapped!

"Get me out!" gasped Percy, going greener by the minute
As the bubble bibble-bobbled **up** and **up**
with **Percy** still within it.

Then, suddenly the hermit crab
dived back into his shell.
"LOOK OUT!" the others cried
—as they tried to hide as well.

"Oh, see those razor teeth," they gasped,
"those evil eyes . . . good grief!
It's Two-Ton Tom the tiger shark,

the **terror** of the reef!"

The tiger shark saw Percy and said, "Yummm, a juicy snack!"
And opened up his massive mouth and moved in to attack!
"Dinner-time!" he laughed,
but just before his jaws could close . . .

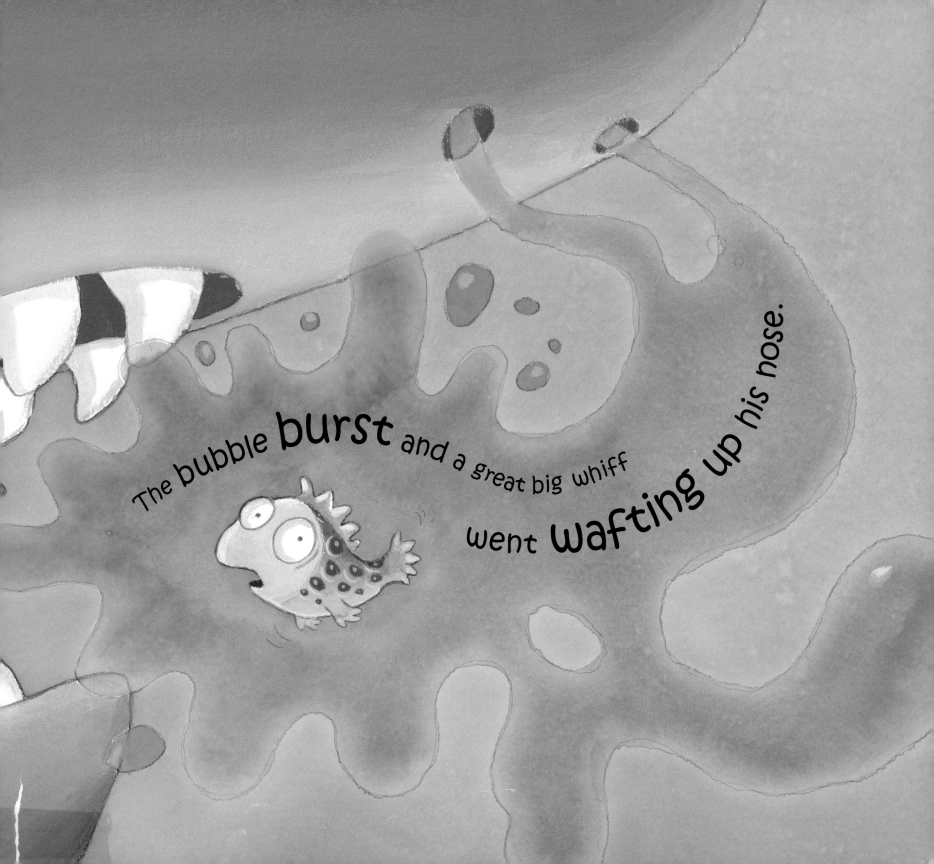

The bubble **burst** and a great big whiff went **wafting up** his nose.

The shark swam off.

"Hooray for Percy!" all the others cried.

And Percy felt a warm and tingly

feeling deep inside.

"You must be feeling proud!"

    suggested Hermit Crab and grinned.

"Well maybe," Percy said. "But, then again it could be...

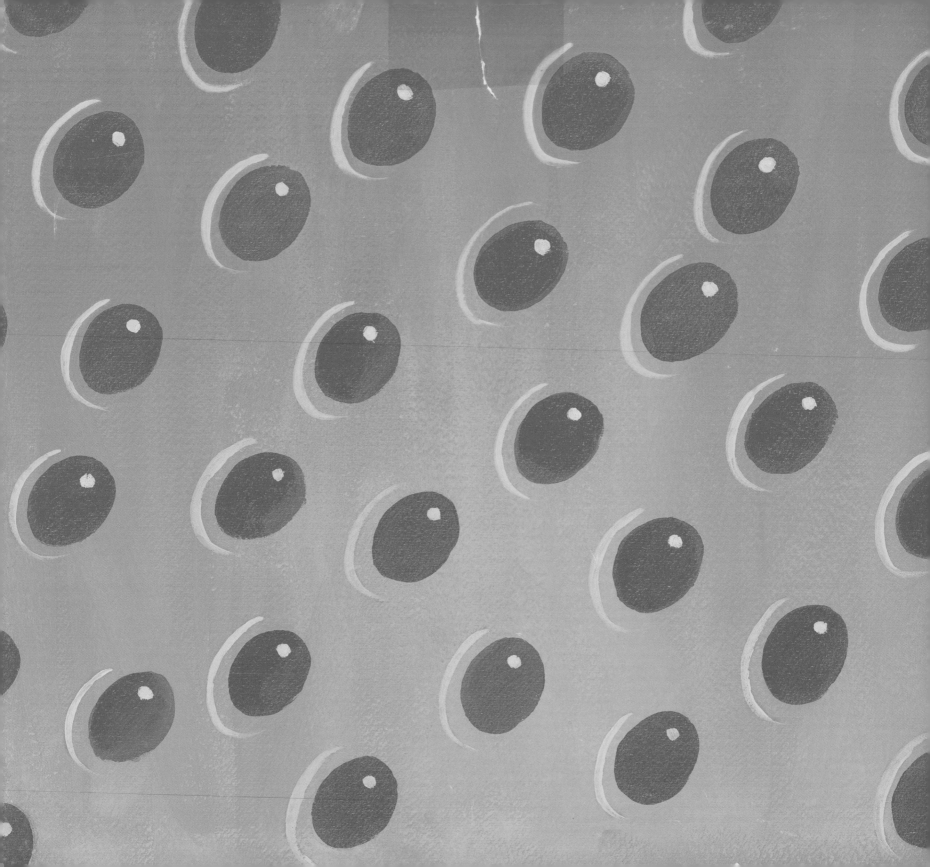